W9-CZY-312

Last Night
I Dreamed a
Circus

by Maya Gottfried
paintings by Robert Rahway Zakanitch

Alfred A. Knopf New York

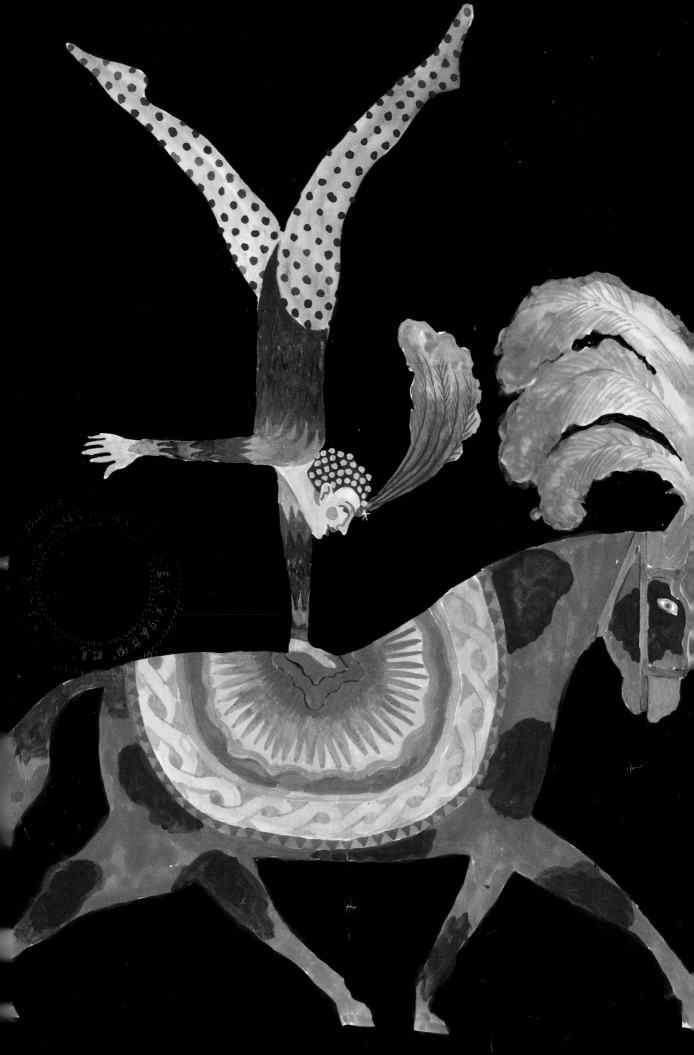

Last night

I dreamed

a circus.

I spun circles

round

the stars.

And juggled a rose garden.

wore the sunset on a velvet cape

And carried the birds

that sang the sky.

I jumped through hoops.

And fell through the air.

And flew.

I twisted in knots.

And I laughed.

And roared.

I rode atop

the elephant

of the seven seas.

And it

carried me home.

Last night

I dreamed

a circus.

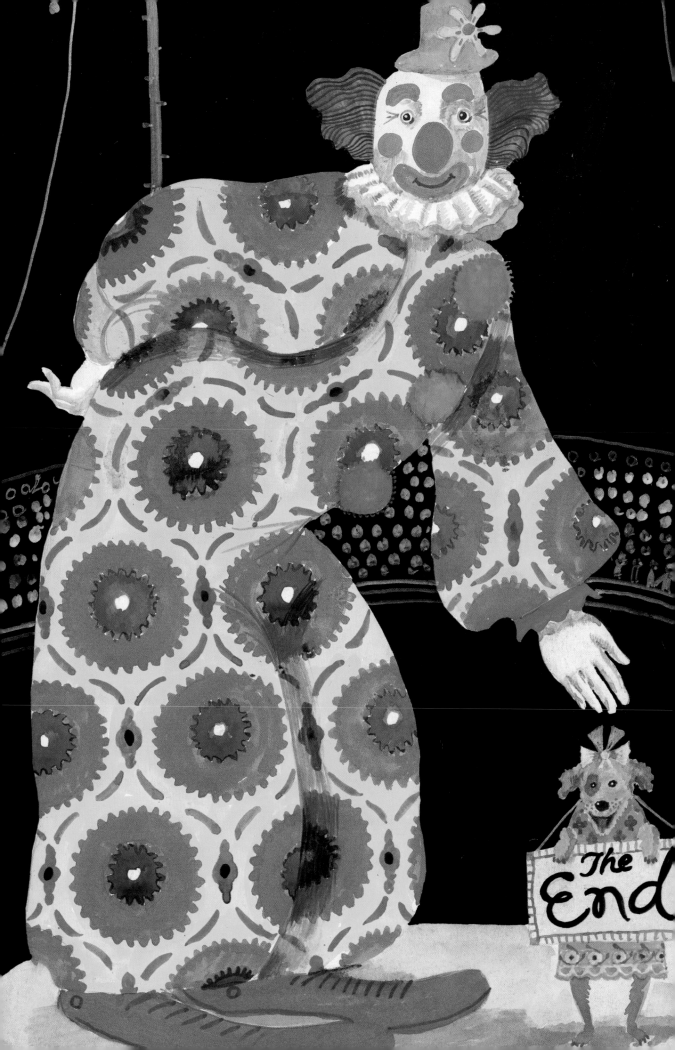

The End

Thank you Mom and Dad for all of your help.
—M.G.

Special thanks to Soaring Gardens Artist Retreat,
to Jane Lahr for her support and perseverance,
and to Maya Gottfried for her gentle and poignant prose.
—R.R.Z.

THIS IS A BORZOI BOOK PUBLISHED BY ALFRED A. KNOPF

Text copyright © 2003 by Maya Gottfried
Illustrations copyright © 2003 by Robert Rahway Zakanitch
All rights reserved under International and Pan-American Copyright Conventions.
Published in the United States by Alfred A. Knopf,
an imprint of Random House Children's Books,
a division of Random House, Inc., New York,
and simultaneously in Canada by Random House of Canada Limited, Toronto.
Distributed by Random House, Inc., New York.
KNOPF, BORZOI BOOKS, and the colophon are registered trademarks of Random House, Inc.

www.randomhouse.com/kids

Library of Congress Cataloging-in-Publication Data
Gottfried, Maya.
Last night I dreamed a circus / by Maya Gottfried; illustrated by Robert Rahway Zakanitch.—1st ed.
p. cm.
"Borzoi Books."
Summary: A young girl dreams of being part of the circus.
[1. Circus—Fiction. 2. Dreams—Fiction.] I. Zakanitch, Robert, 1935–, ill. II. Title.
PZ7.G6945 Las 2003
[E]—dc21 2002030196

ISBN 0-375-82388-3 (trade)
ISBN 0-375-92388-8 (lib. bdg.)

Printed in the United States of America
10 9 8 7 6 5 4 3 2 1
January 2003
First Edition